THIS BOOK BELONGS TO

THE CLASSIC TREASURY OF BULFINCH'S
MYTHOLOGY

ILLUSTRATED BY GILES GREENFIELD · RETOLD BY STEVEN ZORN

COURAGE BOOKS

AN IMPRINT OF RUNNING PRESS
PHILADELPHIA · LONDON

Library of Congress Control Number: 2002108142

ISBN 0-7624-1900-8

Designed by Dustin Summers
Edited by Susan K. Hom
Typography: Charlemagne and Centaur

This book may be ordered by mail from the publisher.
But try your bookstore first!

Published by Courage Books, an imprint of
Running Press Book Publishers
125 South Twenty-second Street
Philadelphia, Pennsylvania 19103-4399

Visit us on the web!

www.runningpress.com

CONTENTS

INTRODUCTION

THE WORLD IS FULL OF MYSTERY: SEASONS CHANGE, PLANTS GROW, BABIES ARE BORN, COUPLES FALL IN LOVE, AND NATIONS GO TO WAR AGAINST EACH OTHER.

To find answers to life's mysteries, the ancient Greeks and Romans invented gods and goddesses. Everything that humans saw or experienced was explained by the whims or plans of these immortal beings.

But the gods and goddess were not perfect. They were often vain and short-tempered, sometimes deceitful, and not always fair with one another. They lived on the summit of Mount Olympus in north-eastern Greece, where they controlled the destiny of mortals and quarreled among themselves. They could change into any creature, but usually took human form.

Although the Greeks and the Romans worshipped the same gods, they called them by different names. The names in this book are Roman.

Besides gods, grotesque monsters in all shapes roamed the unexplored parts of the earth. Nymphs, the peaceable daughter of the gods, inhabited forests, stream, and meadows. Over the years, the nymphs have become the storybook spirits we call fairies.

The tales in this book have been adapted from *The Age of Fable* by Thomas Bulfinch. He wrote it in 1855. Thomas was the son of Charles Bulfinch, the architect of the Capitol Building in Washington, D.C. He was born in Boston, where he taught Latin for a year, and then worked as a bank clerk.

Passionate about the myths of the ancients, Bulfinch wrote *The Age of Fable* to introduce a new generation to these wonderful stories. He later wrote *The Age of Chivalry* and *Legends of Charlemagne*, which retold the tales of medieval times. To this day, Bulfinch's works remain among the most highly regarded books of myths and legends.

THE TROJAN WAR

MINERVA WAS THE GODDESS OF WISDOM, BUT ONE DAY SHE DID A VERY FOOLISH THING:

she entered into a beauty competition with Juno, the queen of the gods, and Venus, the goddess of love. Here's how it happened:

It was the occasion of the most festive wedding ever witnessed—even by the gods. The bride was Thetis, a beautiful sea nymph. Her bridegroom was King Peleus, a mighty—but mortal—warrior. The happy couple invited all of the gods to this spectacular affair. All, that is, except Eris, the goddess of discord.

Would Eris stand for such a slight? Absolutely not! Creating conflict was a game to her; disruption was her talent. She couldn't let such an opportunity pass.

The most dangerous plans are also the most simple, and nothing could surpass the simplicity of Eris's evil scheme. During the wedding feast, she sneaked invisibly into the banquet room and rolled a single golden apple down the long banquet table. On the apple she inscribed the simple words: "To the Fairest."

The gleaming apple stopped right in front of Minerva, Juno, and Venus. The three beautiful and usually dignified goddesses each had a streak of vanity. The apple and its message appealed to their haughty pride. After a moment's hesitation, they lunged after it, each one claiming to be the apple's rightful owner. They began to argue bitterly, but when they realized that none of them would back down, they asked Jupiter, king of all the gods, to choose the fairest. Jupiter, much too wise to make such a delicate decision, suggested that the goddesses pay a visit to young Paris, the prince of Troy, who was a lover of beauty. The goddesses agreed.

Though Paris was indeed a prince, he had no kingdom. Instead, he worked as a common shepherd. His father, the king of Troy, had sent him away because of a prophecy. The king had been warned that his son would bring about the downfall of the kingdom.

The three goddesses appeared before a very startled Paris as he tended his flock. They asked him to decide who should have the apple.

As Paris gazed at the three goddesses, considering his answer, each leaned forward and whispered into his ear, hoping to influence his decision. Juno promised him power and riches. Minerva promised glory and renown in war. Venus promised him the fairest mortal woman for his wife: Queen Helen of Sparta. Paris awarded the apple, which became known as the Apple of Discord, to Venus.

Every eligible man in Greece had sought Helen's hand, and men were willing to kill each other for her. Before that could happen, her suitors took an oath. They promised to protect Helen, no matter whom she wed. She then married King

Menelaus of Sparta. Now Venus promised her to Paris.

Paris, protected by Venus, sailed to Sparta, pretending to be a friend. King Menelaus welcomed him into his home, never expecting Paris to kidnap his wife. Paris kidnapped Helen and took her back to Troy.

Upon the discovery of this treacherous act, the Greek army sent warships to Troy to reclaim the Spartan queen. Helen became known as the face that launched 1,000 ships. The Trojan War had begun— a bloody battle between the world's fiercest armies. Even the gods took sides.

The war between Troy and Greece raged ten years. It would have lasted even longer if not for the crafty Greeks.

In Troy stood a famous statue called the Palladium. It was an enormous figure of Minerva, the goddess of wisdom, and was said to have fallen from heaven. Everyone believed that the city could not be defeated as long as the statue remained within it. No matter how hard the Greeks attacked, Troy would not buckle.

Ulysses and Diomed, two of the great war heroes on the Greek side, plotted to steal the Palladium and end the war. They disguised themselves, sneaked into the walled city of Troy, and snuck out with it under cover of darkness. Then the Greek army attacked the city of Troy once again.

But Troy still held out, and the Greeks began to fear they could never win the kingdom by force. Something more clever was called for, and Ulysses was the one to think of it.

The Greek army pretended to abandon the battle. The generals withdrew most of the troops and hid the warships behind a nearby island. The remaining men built an enormous wooden horse before sailing away.

The Trojans saw that the Greeks were gone and assumed they had given up. The gates of Troy were thrown open and the citizens flooded out, rejoicing at their freedom.

The sight of the empty Greek camp surprised the Trojans. They found the great horse even more astonishing. What could it

be for? Some suggested taking it into the city as a trophy. Others felt afraid of it—and wisely so, because within the belly of the horse hid some of Greece's fiercest warriors.

While the Trojans considered what to do with this strange souvenir, Laocoön, the priest of the sea god Neptune, exclaimed, "Citizens, what madness is this? Have you not learned enough of the Greeks to be on your guard against them? I fear the Greeks, even when they offer gifts."

Laocoön threw his spear against the massive horse, and the statue rang hollow. The Trojans' grew suspicious, but only for a moment. Just then some scouts returned, dragging a Greek prisoner.

They brought the captive before the Trojan chiefs, who promised to spare his life if he answered their questions truthfully.

The sobbing prisoner said his name was Sinon and that he was a soldier in the Greek army under Ulysses's command. Sinon told the Trojans that Ulysses thought he was a coward and had left him behind to die.

But Sinon was far from being a coward. He was a brave Greek warrior, and the story he told was made up by Ulysses to win the Trojans' trust.

Sinon told the Trojans that the Greeks felt they had offended Minerva by stealing the Palladium. The horse was built as a gift to Minerva in hopes of winning back her favor, he explained.

Sinon, a skillful and convincing teller of tales, cried uncontrollably as he went on: they built the horse so huge to prevent it from being carried within the walls of Troy. A prophet had told Ulysses that if the Trojans took it, they would surely win the war.

This news thrilled most of Troy's citizens. Those who still doubted were convinced by what happened next.

The sea god Neptune favored the Greeks over the Trojans. To make Sinon's story even more believable, he sent two enormous sea serpents. The beasts devoured Laocoön and his two sons as the horrified crowd looked on. The Trojans took this as proof that the gods were angered by Laocoön's disrespectful treatment of the sacred horse. Triumphant, they brought the horse into their city amid songs and celebrations.

Later that night, while the people of Troy lay sleeping, overcome by their feast and festivities, Sinon released the horse's deadly cargo. The troops within the horse opened the gates of the city to the rest of the Greek army, which had silently returned.

Troy fell that night, and a long and bloody war was ended.

ULYSSES

IN THEIR HASTE TO RETURN HOME AFTER WINNING THE TROJAN WAR, THE GREEKS FORGOT TO THANK THE GODS FOR THEIR VICTORY. SO THE GODS TURNED AGAINST THEM.

To punish Ulysses, king of Ithaca and hero of the war, the gods created one misadventure after another, delaying his return to his family. Less than a year before the Trojan War had begun, Ulysses had married Penelope, a lovely, intelligent, and devoted woman. Together they had a son, Telemachus. He was only a few weeks old when his father went to war. Once the war ended, the ten year-old boy waited for the return of the father he never knew. But it took ten more years for brave Ulysses to actually arrive back on Ithaca's shores.

One of the first obstacles Ulysses and his crew faced was the Lotus-eaters. This kindly race entertained the men on their island and served them the seeds of the delicate water plant. Those who ate the lotus lost all memory of home and wished to remain on the island. Ulysses was forced to drag his crew away from their hosts and tie each man to the ship so that they could sail.

Next they arrived in the country of the Cyclopes. The name means "round eye," for each of these fearsome giants had a single eye in the middle of his forehead. Ulysses's ships landed on the island and his men came ashore to gather supplies. They

entered a cave, bringing a jug of wine as a gift to whoever lived there. No one was inside, but they found plenty of cheese and pails of milk, well-kept lambs and kids in their pens. As the sailors studied these treasures, the Cyclops entered the cave with a load of firewood. The giant, named Polyphemus, became outraged that the men had come into his home uninvited.

"Who dares to sneak into my home to steal my things?" thundered the giant. "Who are you and where do you come from?" he demanded.

Ulysses replied most humbly. "We are but Greeks, from the great war that brought us such glory," he explained. "We do not wish to steal your food. We ask only for your hospitality. We are trying to make our way home."

"Bah!" shouted Polyphemus. He grabbed two of the men as if they were sticks, and threw them against the side of the cave. Then he devoured them.

Polyphemus made prisoners of Ulysses and his men. Each night, the giant would kill and eat two of them. Finally, Ulysses and his remaining crew managed to blind Polyphemus as the giant slept. They made a fast escape from that terrible island.

But Ulysses's troubles had just begun. Polyphemus was the son of the powerful sea god Neptune. Furious that Ulysses had wounded Polyphemus, Neptune did all he could to prevent Ulysses from reaching home.

Everywhere the ships landed, danger awaited. On the beautiful isle of Aeaea, the crew found themselves surrounded by lions, wolves, and tigers. The men were surprised to discover that the beasts were all tame as puppies. The real danger was a powerful magician named Circe, who had put the wild animals under a spell. Circe seemed to be a gracious host. She prepared tempting meals for the men, sang to them, made certain they were comfortable—and then she turned them into pigs!

Mercury, the messenger god, helped Ulysses rescue his men. After that, Circe promised no more tricks, and warned

Ulysses of the dangers that lay ahead once he left the island.

Among these dangers were the Sirens, creatures with the bodies of birds and the faces of beautiful women. They lived on a rocky coast and sang a song irresistible to any man. Sailors hearing their melody would dive into the sea and drown.

Circe told Ulysses to put wax in his crew's ears and have them tie him to the mast so that he could hear, but be unable to obey, the songs of death.

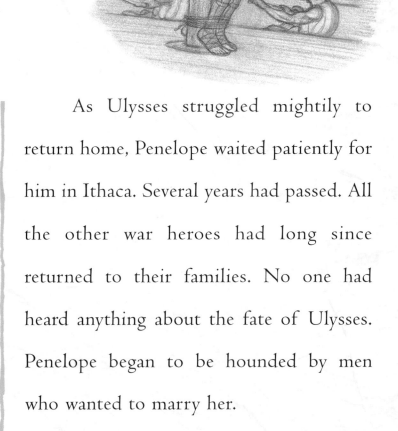

The sea was calm as the sailors approached the Sirens' island. Over the glassy waters came notes so attractive that tears streamed down Ulysses's face as he struggled to get loose. He begged his men to release him, but they only tied him tighter. They held the ship on course and the music grew fainter until Ulysses could not hear it at all. At last he stopped struggling and, with a nod of his head, he gave his companions the signal to unseal their ears and untie him.

As Ulysses struggled mightily to return home, Penelope waited patiently for him in Ithaca. Several years had passed. All the other war heroes had long since returned to their families. No one had heard anything about the fate of Ulysses. Penelope began to be hounded by men who wanted to marry her.

"The war has been over a great while," one of the men said. "If Ulysses is not home by now, he is most certainly dead."

Some of the suitors were officers who had returned from the Trojan War. Others were noblemen from neighboring kingdoms who, by marrying Penelope, could take over Ulysses's kingdom and expand their own land.

These uninvited, unwelcome guests moved into Penelope's home, slaughtered and ate her cattle and sheep, and refused to leave until Penelope chose a new husband. They treated young Telemachus like a servant and even threatened to carry Penelope off if she did not choose a husband soon.

Penelope's faith in Ulysses never wavered. She knew that her husband would one day return to reclaim his kingdom. She did what she could to avoid being forced into remarriage.

She remained friendly to the suitors, letting them think that she was considering marrying one of them. This tactic worked for a long time, but then the men grew impatient and demanded an answer.

Penelope created a clever plan. She told the suitors that she would remarry, but only after she finished knitting an elaborate burial cloth for Ulysses's father, now a very old man. Though the suitors were brutes, they could not deny Penelope this sacred task.

By day, Penelope wove together the threads of the exquisite cloth, but each night she would secretly unravel it by torchlight. She kept this up for more than three years before the suitors discovered her trick.

All the while, Ulysses battled the gods so that he could return to her. The only route home was through a narrow passage between a great whirlpool called Charybdis and a huge, six-headed snake known as Scylla. To avoid catastrophe, the ship had to sail perfectly between these two perils.

Ulysses kept strict watch as his crew steered. The roar of the waters warned that the ship was nearing Charybdis, but Ulysses could see no sign of Scylla. As he and his men anxiously watched for the dreaded whirlpool, the horrific serpent darted forth her snaky heads and carried six shrieking crewmen to her watery den.

Deeply saddened by the loss of their friends, the men sailed on and faced many other dangers. Only Ulysses survived all the hardships placed before him by the gods.

Just as Penelope began to lose hope of ever seeing him again, Ulysses reached Ithaca. With the help of Telemachus, now a young man, he rid his house of the suitors and was reunited with his wife.

Ulysses proved that one person's determination can be stronger than the anger of all the gods.

KING MIDAS

KING MIDAS WAS A FAIR RULER, BUT HIS UNWISE WORDS ALWAYS GOT HIM INTO TROUBLE.

Once, Midas played host to a jolly old deity named Silenus. Silenus was absentminded and had a habit of wandering off. That's how he came to be in Midas's kingdom in the first place. In his younger days, Silenus had taught winemaking to Bacchus, the wine god. Now Bacchus took care of his old master. He was very upset when Silenus disappeared. But Midas was a gracious host, and after a few days, returned Silenus to a grateful Bacchus.

The wine god, overjoyed that no harm had come to his master, offered Midas whatever he might wish. The king didn't pause to think before replying: "I wish for all I touch to be turned to gold."

Bacchus granted the wish, but he was sorry that Midas had not made a better choice.

Midas hastened to put his new power to the test. He plucked a branch from an oak and it turned to gold. He picked up a rock, and it too became gold.

It was true! The king could scarcely believe his good fortune. After several

hours of gold-making, the king worked up quite an appetite. He went home to a splendid meal. At first he was amused when he reached for the bread and it turned to gold. But when the same thing happened to his wine, then to his salad, and then to his meat, Midas grew horrified.

His wish had become a curse; starvation seemed to await him. He hated his gift and prayed for Bacchus to remove it. Bacchus heard him and consented.

"Go" said Bacchus, "to the River Pactolus. Plunge in and wash away your power."

Midas jumped into the river and his gold-making ability passed into the waters. Even today, gold may be found among the sands of that river.

After such a terrible experience, Midas rejected wealth and moved to the country to live a simple life. There he worshipped Pan, the bearded, cloven-hoofed god of the fields who played wonderful tunes on reed pipes.

One day, Pan challenged the mighty Apollo, god of the sun and also god of music, to a musical competition. Midas was one of the judges.

Pan blew his reeds beautifully; Apollo chose the lyre, and played with superb skill. When it came time to judge, everyone but Midas agreed that Apollo's music was sweeter. Midas stubbornly declared, "Apollo played no better than Pan. My fellow judges favor Apollo not for his skill but because he is the more powerful of the two gods. I think that Pan is the better musician."

Apollo, enraged that Midas would question his talent, bellowed that Midas's hearing was coarse and untrained. To prove his point, Apollo turned the king's ears into those of a mule.

The king's long hair hid his shame from all but his barber, who was sworn to secrecy. But such a juicy secret is hard to keep. He had to let it out. Frustrated, the barber went to a meadow and dug a deep hole. He whispered the story into the hole and buried it. But that didn't put an end to it.

Before long, a thick patch of reeds sprung up at that spot. Whenever the wind blew, the reeds could be heard to whisper "the king has mule's ears . . . the king has mule's ears . . . . "

ORPHEUS AND EURYDICE

C AN LOVE CONQUER DEATH?
ORPHEUS BELIEVED SO.

Orpheus was the son of Apollo, the sun god who was also the god of music. His mother, the goddess Calliope, inspired mortals to write poetry. With these two parents, is it any wonder that Orpheus was the greatest singer that ever lived? When he was a young boy, his father had given him a stringed instrument called a lyre and taught him to play it. Orpheus played with such perfection that wild beasts would peacefully gather around him, trees would pull up their roots and follow him, and even rocks would soften to the strains of his instrument and the tender words he sang.

More than music or even life itself, Orpheus loved a woman named Eurydice. The two were married only a short time when tragedy struck.

One day, as Eurydice wandered through a field, a shepherd became entranced by her charm and began to chase her. Fleeing from him, Eurydice stepped on a snake. The snake bit her on the foot, and she died.

Orpheus could not contain his grief over the loss of his bride. He sang prayers to the gods and poured out his sorrow to his friends, but nothing eased his sadness.

At last he decided he must visit Tartarus, the land of the dead. There, he hoped to make a heartfelt plea to Pluto, lord of the underworld, for the return of his wife. Orpheus would risk everything to bring her back.

Tartarus was a kingdom of horrors. Those who had committed crimes during their lifetimes paid for those crimes forever. Terrifying monsters made certain that all who entered could never escape. Orpheus felt he must try.

The passage to Tartarus was through a cave filled with the demons Grief, Worry, Disease, Age, Fear, Hunger, Toil, Poverty,

and Death, in forms too dreadful to view. Fire-breathing Chimeras, and nine-headed, hissing Hydras lurked in the darkness. Also prowling were the Furies, hideous sister goddesses who tormented anyone who had committed a crime that had not been discovered.

Beyond this passage, more horrors awaited. But Orpheus would not turn back. All the demons of Tartarus could not equal the pain of life without Eurydice.

Orpheus came to the bank of a black river where thousands of passengers waited anxiously to be ferried across. Charon, the ferryman, chose only those who had received a proper burial.

"While you still live, you cannot be my passenger," spoke Charon, in a voice chilling to hear.

"I come to seek my wife, whom you brought across this dark, sad river only a short time ago. Please let me find her," Orpheus pleaded. He then sang a song of Eurydice, comparing the depths of his love for her to the bottomless depths of Charon's river.

The song won Charon's sympathy. He allowed Orpheus to board his craft. It groaned under the weight of its live passenger. At last he was in Tartarus, which was guarded by Cerberus, a ferocious, three-headed dog. Orpheus sang the dog to sleep and entered the gate.

First he heard the wailing of children and of people who had been wrongly executed. Then he passed into the region of sadness, where heartbroken lovers were not freed from pain even by death. Orpheus found himself before the thrones of Pluto and Proserpine, the king and queen of Tartarus.

"What mortal dares to visit the haunts of the dead while he himself still breathes?" demanded Pluto.

"Oh gods of the underworld," sang Orpheus, as he played his lyre, "hear my words, for they are true. I do not wish to learn your secrets, nor to defy you. I come to seek my wife, whose years were ended by a viper's fang.

"Love has led me here," Orpheus sang, "Love, a god all-powerful with us who live on earth, and who is just as powerful here.

"I beg you to return to life my wife Eurydice. We all must come to you some day, but please let Eurydice live a full life before she must dwell here forever."

As Orpheus sang, the ghosts began to cry. Sisyphus, who had been sentenced to forever roll a huge boulder up a steep hill—only to have it roll down again, over and over—sat against the rock to listen.

Tantalus, cursed with unquenchable thirst and gnawing hunger for betraying Zeus, heard the words and felt satisfied.

Even the hideous, cruel faces of the Furies were wet with tears. Proserpine could not deny Orpheus's request, and Pluto called for Eurydice. She appeared from among the recently arrived spirits, limping on her wounded foot.

"You may take her back to earth on one condition," said Pluto. "She is to follow behind you, and you must not look back at her until you are both in daylight again."

Orpheus agreed.

Orpheus and Eurydice began their slow and horrifying escape from the land of the dead. Throughout, Orpheus remained a few steps ahead of his wife.

As they neared the mouth of the cave, a ray of daylight beamed in. They had nearly reached the outlet when, in a moment of forgetfulness, Orpheus turned to glance behind him. But Eurydice had not yet entered the light. Instantly, an unseen force whisked her back into the cavern's awful depths. The couple stretched out their arms for one last embrace, but clasped only the air.

"Farewell," cried Eurydice, dying a second time, "a last farewell," and she was gone.

MEDUSA, PEGASUS, AND THE CHIMERA

P

ERSEUS WAS THE SON OF THE GOD JUPITER AND A MORTAL WOMAN. HE HAD A HEROIC LIFE, BUT NOT A HAPPY BEGINNING.

When he was born, a prophecy foretold that he would one day cause the death of his mortal grandfather. (Later in his life, Perseus would accidentally kill his grandfather with a discus.) To prevent that from happening, his grandfather shut the infant Perseus and his mother in a chest and sent it adrift on the ocean.

The chest floated a great distance until a fisherman found it and rescued Perseus and his mother. The fisherman took them to his king, who treated them well. Perseus grew to be a young man, and the king sent him to conquer a monster named Medusa, who had terrorized the country.

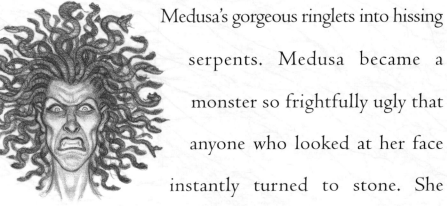

Once a beautiful maiden with shiny, flowing locks of hair, Medusa dared to compare her beauty with that of Minerva. As punishment, the goddess of wisdom changed Medusa's gorgeous ringlets into hissing serpents. Medusa became a monster so frightfully ugly that anyone who looked at her face instantly turned to stone. She lived in a cave, surrounded by the stony figures of animals and people who had had the misfortune to catch a glimpse of her.

One night, while Medusa slept, Perseus entered the cave. He sneaked care-

fully inside, using a shiny shield as a mirror to avoid looking directly at Medusa. When he found her, he cut off her head and presented it to Minerva as a gift.

The blood from Medusa's wound created the winged horse Pegasus, who was caught and tamed by Minerva. Pegasus later helped to defeat another monster called the Chimera. Here's how it happened:

The Chimera was a fearsome, fire-breathing monster. The front of its body was a combination of a lion and a goat; the hind part was a dragon. It raised havoc in the country of Lycia, and the king sought someone to destroy it.

A young warrior named Bellerophon came to Lycia, and the king asked him to kill the beast, even though no one believed it could be done. But Bellerophon never considered the danger and he couldn't deny the king's request.

Before going into combat with the Chimera, Bellerophon visited a prophet. The prophet told him that to succeed, he must ride Pegasus. He suggested that Bellerophon spend a night in the temple of Minerva, because she still kept the winged steed. Bellerophon did as the prophet told him. As he slept in the temple, Minerva visited him in a dream. In the dream, she gave him a golden bridle, and showed him where he could find Pegasus.

When he awoke, Bellerophon still held the bridle. Grateful that the gods had blessed him, he went to the place he had dreamed of and there he found the wonderful steed drinking from a fountain. At the sight of the bridle, Pegasus eagerly trotted over to his new master.

Bellerophon rode Pegasus to victory over the Chimera. It was the first of many victories they shared.

HERCULES

JUPITER, KING OF THE GODS, HAD SEVERAL MORTAL CHILDREN. HIS MOST FAMOUS CHILD WAS HERCULES, THE STRONGEST MAN ON EARTH. JUPITER'S WIFE, JUNO, DIDN'T LIKE HER HUSBAND'S HUMAN CHILDREN.

She especially disliked Hercules because even though he was mortal, he had the strength of a god.

Juno believed that Hercules would only cause trouble as he grew older and stronger, so she waged war on him almost from the moment of his birth. When he was just a few weeks old, Juno sent two snakes to destroy him as he lay in his cra-dle. But already he proved he was some-thing special: baby Hercules strangled the serpents with his bare hands.

As Hercules grew to manhood, Juno continued testing him, and Hercules always passed the tests. This enraged the queen of the gods. Finally, she ordered Hercules to perform a series of dangerous tasks, which became known as the Twelve

Labors of Hercules. Jupiter allowed Juno to order Hercules to perform the labors. He felt confident that his son could pass these tests, and he believed that Hercules would be an inspiration to other mortals.

Most of the labors involved killing ferocious animals, like the Nemean Lion and the Hydra.

The Nemean Lion, a ferocious beast, terrorized the valley of Nemea. When clubs and arrows proved useless against it, Hercules used his childhood trick and choked it to death with his bare hands.

The Hydra, a nine-headed monster, lived in a swamp. Its middle head was immortal, meaning it could never be killed. When any of the hydra's other eight heads were cut off, two would instantly grow back. The more the creature was cut, the more dangerous it became.

For this labor, Hercules had help from his faithful servant Iolaus. As each of the Hydra's heads was chopped off, the two men burned the wound with a flaming torch so they couldn't grow back. Then Hercules and Iolaus buried the immortal head under a boulder.

Hercules next faced a much less dangerous but much dirtier job. A king named Augeas had a herd of 3,000 oxen whose stables had not been cleaned for 30 years. Hercules was ordered to thoroughly clean each stall, a task that could easily take years to finish. The disgusting and humiliating assignment was hardly fit for a hero, but Hercules handled it in truly heroic fashion. Rather than shoveling the colossal mountains of filth, Hercules changed the courses of two nearby rivers. The flowing water ran through the stables and flushed them clean. He finished the job in a single day. It only proves what a little ingenuity and a lot of brute strength can accomplish.

Hercules's next labor was more delicate. He had to obtain a belt that belonged to the queen of the Amazons.

The Amazons were a nation of warrior women. They raised only female babies and sent boys away to neighboring kingdoms. Hercules went to their island and received a warm welcome by Queen Hippolyta. Amused that Hercules had traveled so far only for her belt, she presented it to him as a gift.

Juno, angry that this labor had gone so smoothly, took the form of an Amazon and persuaded the other Amazons that Hercules's true mission was to carry off Hippolyta.

The Amazons, rushing to rescue their queen, attacked Hercules's crew. Hercules, thinking that Hippolyta had betrayed him, slew her before sailing off with her belt.

Hercules's most difficult labor was gathering the golden apples of the Hesperides.

The apples had been given to Juno as a wedding present from the goddess of the earth. Three sisters, known as the Hesperides, guarded them.

The Hesperides were the daughters of Atlas, a giant from a race older than the gods, called the Titans. Long ago, the Titans and the gods fought for control of the universe. The gods won and punished the Titans. For Atlas's punishment, he had to bear the weight of the earth upon his shoulders forever.

Hercules didn't know where to find the Hesperides, so he asked Atlas to get the apples for him. Atlas was eager to be relieved of his burden for a while, and Hercules was the only person strong enough for the job of holding the earth. Atlas collected the apples, gave them to Hercules, and reluctantly took the earth upon his shoulders once again.

Another celebrated exploit of Hercules was his victory over Antaeus. Antaeus, the son of Terra, the Earth, was a mighty giant and wrestler. He remained invincible as long as he stayed in contact with mother Earth. He forced any strangers coming into his country to wrestle with him. If they lost—and they always did—they paid with their lives.

Hercules, as one of his labors, challenged Antaeus. As they fought, Hercules found it useless to throw the giant to the ground because he always rose again with greater strength. Finally, Hercules lifted him up high above his head, so Antaeus couldn't touch the earth. There, holding him in mid-air, Hercules strangled him to death.

One by one, Hercules successfully completed each of his twelve tasks. His bravery impressed even Juno, and her heart softened. Finally he won the queen's friendship and was granted immortality.

DAEDALUS AND ICARUS

ON THE ISLE OF CRETE LIVED A BRUTAL MONSTER CALLED THE MINOTAUR.

It had a bull's muscular body, a grotesque, barely human face, horns, and sharp teeth. It was extremely strong and fierce.

Minos, the king of Crete, kept the Minotaur in a maze built by Daedalus, a master craftsman. The Minotaur's maze was artfully designed. With its numberless winding passages, twists, and turns, it seemed to have neither beginning nor end.

Minos ruled with great cruelty. He ordered that each year seven young men and seven young women be sent to their deaths by locking them in the maze. Within its twisted corridors the Minotaur roamed, waiting for its next meal of human flesh.

The friendship of an evil king cannot be trusted. Soon after building the maze, Daedalus lost the king's favor. Minos condemned him and his young son Icarus to live in the maze until the Minotaur found and devoured them.

So perfect was the maze that even its builder could not escape from its tangled halls. Still, Daedalus planned his escape. He knew he could not leave the island by sea because Minos searched every ship.

"Minos may control the land and sea," said Daedalus, "but not the air. I will try that way."

Daedalus gathered feathers, which he fastened together with bits of string and globs of wax. Young Icarus would chase after the feathers that blew away, or he would sit by his father and play with the wax.

Before long, Daedalus had completed two sets of wings. He strapped one set to himself and, flapping them gently, began to rise gracefully. With a little practice, Daedalus could fly forward and backward, and suspend himself in air. Next, he fitted Icarus with the other pair of wings and taught the excited boy to master them.

When the two were ready to fly beyond the walls of their prison, Daedalus spoke with a trembling voice:

"Icarus, my son, you must remember not to fly too high, for the heat of the sun can melt your wings. Keep near me and you will be safe."

Daedalus rose slowly into the air, and Icarus followed behind. Occasionally the father would glance back to see his boy's progress. As they flew, the plowman stopped his work to gaze and the shepherd leaned on his staff to watch them, astonished at the sight and thinking them to be gods.

Thrilled by the feeling of freedom, Icarus forgot his father's words and began to soar upward as if to reach heaven. The blazing sun softened the wax that held the feathers together. One by one they began

to drop away. Icarus wildly waved his arms, but no feathers remained to pin him to the air.

"Father!" he cried, as he plunged into the sea.

"Icarus, Icarus, where are you?" his father shouted. At last he looked down and saw the remains of his child's wings floating on the Aegean Sea.

In his son's memory, Daedalus named the spot the Icarian Sea. It has been called that ever since.

CUPID AND PSYCHE

BEAUTY WAS A CURSE TO A YOUNG WOMAN NAMED PSYCHE. SHE WAS SO LOVELY THAT PEOPLE TRAVELED GREAT DISTANCES JUST TO LOOK AT HER.

Venus, the goddess of love, was jealous of Psyche's beauty and the attention she received from her admirers. She often complained to her son, Cupid, about it. Cupid, a mischievous young god with golden curls and white wings, caused men and women to fall in love by shooting them with his magic arrows.

Venus one day told her son, "My boy, Psyche's beauty gives me great pain.

My temples are empty because men flock to her. Punish her and give your mother a sweet revenge. Make her fall in love with some unworthy soul so that she may embarrass herself and disgrace her family."

To carry out this plan, Cupid visited Psyche while she slept. Psyche was so beautiful that Cupid felt a twinge of pity for her. He sprinkled bitter water on her lips to spoil her future happiness, and then he

pricked her with his arrow to make her fall in love.

At the touch of the arrow, Psyche awoke and looked directly at Cupid. The impish god was invisible, but Psyche's bright eyes startled him. In his confusion, Cupid accidentally jabbed himself with his own arrow without realizing it.

His compassion for Psyche grew, and he sprinkled sweet water upon her hair to undo his spell. He had fallen completely in love with her.

Venus tended to Cupid's wound. She now hated Psyche more than ever. Venus made sure that even though Psyche remained popular, no man would ask for her hand.

Years dragged on, leaving Psyche in utter loneliness. Tired of her beauty and saddened by her solitude, she began to believe she would never be married. Her parents thought she might have somehow angered the gods. They asked the advice of a prophet, who said:

"Psyche will be the bride of no mortal lover. Her future husband awaits her on the top of the mountain. He is a monster whom neither gods nor men can resist."

Her parents were horrified, but Psyche said to them:

"This is my fate for being compared to Venus. Lead me to the mountain where my miserable destiny awaits."

Psyche was brought to the mountain. Panting with fear, her eyes full of tears, she stood alone to face whatever horror might come. Suddenly a breeze lifted her up and brought her to a flowery meadow in front of a magnificent palace.

Hesitantly, she entered. Inside the palace was everything she could have wished for. She saw no one, but a voice addressed her, saying:

"Good lady, we whose voices you hear are your servants, and we shall obey your commands with the utmost care."

Suddenly, her fate didn't seem so

bad. Still, she remained cautious, not knowing what her host might have in store for her.

Tired from her adventure, Psyche went to her chamber to rest. When she wanted dinner, she saw the table magically set without the aid of any servant.

Psyche didn't know it, but the palace was the home of Cupid. He came to visit her each night and was always gone by morning. Psyche never saw his face, and only knew that he was gentle and caring. She soon grew to love him and began to think of him as her husband. She often begged him to stay and let her see him, but he always refused.

"Why should you wish to behold me?" Cupid asked. "Have you any doubt of my love? Have you any wish ungratified? If you saw me, perhaps you would fear me, perhaps adore me," Cupid continued, "but all I ask is to love me."

This satisfied Psyche for a while. Then she began to think about her family who didn't know her fate. One night she asked Cupid to send for her two sisters so they could see that all was well.

Psyche's sisters came and saw Psyche's splendid home. They asked what her husband was like, and she had to admit that she'd never seen him.

"Remember," warned one of the sisters, "the prophet said you would marry a monster. People who live in this valley say your husband is a serpent who will fatten you up and then devour you."

"Take our advice," said her other sister; "keep a lamp and a sharp knife near your bed. When your husband is sound asleep, light the lamp and look at him. If he is a monster, cut off his head."

At first Psyche rejected her sisters' advice, but soon their words haunted her, and her own curiosity grew too strong to resist.

One night, as Cupid lay sleeping, Psyche lit the lamp and held it to her husband's face. What she saw was not some hideous monster, but the most beautiful of the gods, with golden ringlets wandering over his pale neck, and with two magnificent wings, white as snow, on his shoulders.

As Psyche leaned forward to get a closer look, a few drops of burning oil from the lamp fell on the god's shoulder. His eyes sprung open, and without saying a word, Cupid flew out the window.

Psyche ran from the house to follow him, but she stumbled and fell in the dust.

Cupid, turning to look at her, said, "Foolish Psyche, is this how you repay my love? Return to your sisters, whose advice you think is better than mine. I punish you by leaving you forever. Love cannot dwell with suspicion."

Cupid flew off, and the house and gardens vanished with him.

Psyche did not return to her parents' home. Instead she wandered the land, searching for Cupid.

One morning, she spied a magnificent temple upon a lofty mountain. "Perhaps my love lives there," she thought, and rushed toward it.

Inside she found a jumble of corn, barley, wheat, and a variety of farm tools.

Psyche went to work straightening up the temple, believing that she shouldn't neglect any of the gods. The temple belonged to Ceres, the goddess of the harvest. Pleased by Psyche's work, Ceres said:

"Psyche, you are truly worthy of my help. Though I can't protect you from Venus, I can tell you how to win her favor. It is she who is keeping your husband from you. Seek Venus and modestly ask her forgiveness. Perhaps then you and Cupid shall be reunited."

Psyche went to the temple of Venus and prayed to the goddess. The goddess appeared and led Psyche to a huge pigeon coop, which contained piles of assorted beans and seeds.

Venus told Psyche that she must separate all of the grains by evening. Psyche, knowing the task was impossible, sat and wept. But Cupid was watching. He ordered the ants to separate the pile grain by grain. By twilight the job was done.

When Venus returned, she was furious.

"This was no work of yours, wicked

one!" shouted the goddess of love. "I have another task for you."

The next morning, Venus led Psyche to a river. On the other side stood an enormous flock of sheep with golden wool. Venus commanded Psyche to collect a bit of golden fleece from each sheep.

Psyche went to the riverside to follow the order. But the river god said, "Oh maiden, do not try to cross this raging river nor approach the sheep on the other side. The river is at its roughest now, and the rams are at their wildest. Wait until noon; then you may cross the water safely, and you will find the woolly gold sticking to the bushes and trunks of the trees.

Psyche waited and followed these wise words. Her task accomplished, she returned to Venus with her arms full of the golden fleece.

"I know very well that you could not have done this task by yourself," said Venus. "But I have another task, one that you must do completely on your own. Take this box," ordered Venus, "and give it to

Proserpine, the queen of the underworld. Tell her that I have sent you to collect a little of her beauty, for I have lost mine through worrying about my son."

Psyche was certain that this was to be the end of her. Few mortals had ever entered the land of the dead and then returned. She climbed a high cliff and prepared to jump, thinking this was the fastest way to the underworld, when a voice said:

"Poor unlucky girl, what cowardice you show! Why do you think the gods who have helped you thus far would abandon you now?"

The voice told Psyche of a safe passage to the underworld, and warned:

"When Proserpine has given you the box filled with her beauty, you must never open it."

Psyche did as she was told and completed her brave errand. When she was back among the living, she thought it would please her husband if she put a little of Proserpine's divine beauty on her own cheeks. She opened the box. It contained not beauty but deep sleep. Psyche fell to the ground, overcome by drowsiness.

Cupid, seeing what had happened, flew to the spot where Psyche lay. He drew the sleep from her body and put it back in the box. "Again," said he, "you have almost perished by your curiosity. But still I love you."

Cupid then flew to Olympus, where the gods lived, and presented himself to Jupiter, the ruler of them all. He told Jupiter of his undying love for Psyche and asked him to help persuade his mother that Psyche would be a worthy wife. Jupiter agreed to help, and Venus consented to the marriage.

Psyche was brought before all the gods and was handed a cup of ambrosia, the food of the gods.

"Drink this, Psyche," said Jupiter, "and become immortal."

In this way, Psyche became a goddess, and she and Cupid became united forever.

BAUCIS AND PHILEMON

THE GODS WERE OFTEN DEVILISH, BUT THEY COULD ALSO BE COMPASSIONATE.

One night, two weary travelers wandered from door to door in a small village. They looked for food and shelter for the night, but the hour was late and no one would answer their knocking.

At last, the sad travelers came to a simple, thatched hut. The residents, an elderly couple, welcomed them in. Baucis and her husband Philemon had been together since they were young. They were poor, but not ashamed of their poverty. They lived by themselves in this simple shack, never asking for anything more.

As the two guests bowed their heads to pass under the low door, old Philemon pulled out a bench. Baucis, bustling and attentive, spread a cloth upon it and bid them to sit down.

They had very little to offer the strangers, but Baucis and Philemon were free with what they did have.

As Baucis kindled a fire, Philemon prepared some herbs and bacon for a stew.

Baucis, with her apron on and her old hands trembling, set the table. One table leg was shorter than the rest, but a piece of slate set it right. Upon it she set some olives, radishes and cheese, with eggs lightly cooked in the ashes of the fire. When all was ready, Philemon set the stew, smoking hot, on the table. He poured some wine from an earthenware pitcher into their wooden cups. For dessert, they had apples and wild honey. The strangers were given cushions to sit on, and the four enjoyed their modest meal and each other's friendly company.

As the meal went on, the old couple realized with astonishment that the pitcher of wine refilled itself as fast as it was poured. Struck with terror, Baucis and Philemon realized their guests were not weary travelers, but gods.

Falling upon their knees, they begged forgiveness for their humble hospitality. To honor the gods, they offered to make a sacrifice of an old goose that they kept as guardian of their hut, but the bird was too nimble and scurried about, avoiding capture. At last it took shelter between the gods themselves.

The two gods forbade the slaughter of the goose. They revealed themselves to be Jupiter and his son, Mercury, and they told the couple:

"This inhospitable village shall pay the penalty for its disrespect; you alone shall be saved. Come with us to the top of yonder hill."

Baucis and Philemon, accompanied by the gods, labored up the steep incline. When they were near the top, they looked back and saw their village sunken in a lake, with only their own house left standing.

As they lamented the fate of their

neighbors, their old house was changed into a temple: columns replaced the corner posts, the thatched roof became gold, the floors became marble, and the doors were enriched with carving and ornamentation.

"Excellent old man, and woman worthy of such a husband," spoke Jupiter, "what favor have you to ask of us?"

Philemon spoke quietly with Baucis for a few moments, then answered, "We wish to be the guardians of your temple for as long as we may live.

"Also, since we have passed our lives in love with one another, we wish that when we die, it will be at the same moment, so that I may not live to see my wife's grave, nor be lain in my own by her."

Their prayer was granted and they lived for many years as keepers of the temple.

When grown very old, they stood one day before the steps of their great building, telling the story of the place. As they spoke, Baucis saw Philemon begin to sprout leaves, while Philemon saw Baucis changing as well. Soon a leafy crown grew over their heads.

"Farewell dear spouse," they said together, and at the same moment bark closed over their mouths. They had become two trees whose intertwining branches were a living monument to their lifelong love.

ATALANTA

In the ancient world, where men were brave and heroic, and women delicate and beautiful, there lived Atalanta, a woman who had both beauty and strength.

Atalanta was a princess, but for reasons unknown, her father abandoned her on a mountaintop while she was an infant. The gods smiled upon baby Atalanta and sent a she-bear to nurse her. The clan of bears raised her and taught her to hunt and defend herself. She grew to be a natural athlete, whose long, slender legs could carry her swiftly and quietly through her forest home. She could spring like a panther, outrun a deer. To build her strength, she playfully wrestled her childhood friends, the bears. She also taught herself archery and became a first-class shot.

But soon Atalanta yearned to join her own people. The proper Greek women would have nothing to do with her—how could they accept a woman who wrestled bears for fun? What could they say to a woman who felt no need for makeup or fine gowns or jewelry? They could never accept Atalanta—but in truth, Atalanta wasn't very fond of them, either. She had more in common with the Greek men.

At first the men objected when Atalanta joined their tournaments and hunts, but it soon became obvious to everyone that her skills were almost god-like. Atalanta earned the men's respect and they let her participate.

Her most famous adventure was the hunt for the Calydonian Boar. This wild beast of enormous size was destroying the countryside. Its eyes shone with blood and fire, its bristles stood out like spears, and its tusks were like those of an Indian elephant.

Meleager, the prince of Calydon, summoned all the heroes of Greece to help destroy this monster. With them came Atalanta. A buckle of polished gold clasped her vest, an ivory quiver hung from her left shoulder, and her left hand bore her bow. As soon as he saw her, Meleager loved her. Atalanta felt the same stirrings for him. Of all the heroes chasing the Calydonian boar that day, only Atalanta's arrow managed to wound it. Together, she

and Meleagar killed the beast. Then Meleager gave Atalanta the creature's head and hide as a trophy.

The couple's happiness was not meant to be. The Destinies, three dreaded sisters who weave, measure, and cut the thread of life, decided that Meleager's life would be short. Soon after the great hunt, he was dead.

A prophet had once told Atalanta: "Do not marry. Marriage will be your ruin." Having lost the man she loved, Atalanta took the prophecy to heart. She fled from society and devoted herself to hunting and running. But she was not so easily forgotten. Many suitors sought her hand. She impatiently refused every one of them. To regain her privacy, Atalanta made this condition:

"I will marry the man who shall conquer me in a footrace; but death must be the penalty of all who lose."

Many suitors felt it was worth the risk. They gathered to race her. A man named Hippomenes volunteered to judge

the contest. He said to the runners, "How can you men want to risk so much for a wife?" But when he saw Atalanta getting ready for the race, he changed his mind. "Pardon me, youths," he said, "I didn't know the prize you were competing for."

As he watched the race, he looked over the runners and wished Atalanta would beat them all. He swelled with envy if any one of them seemed likely to win. While he thought these thoughts, Atalanta darted forward, looking more beautiful than ever. The breezes seemed to give wings to her feet; her hair flew over her shoulders, the fringe of her garment fluttered behind her, and her pale cheeks flushed crimson. Atalanta speedily outpaced all of her suitors, and each was quickly put to death without mercy.

Even so, Hippomenes, in love with Atalanta, was not afraid to race against her. Looking at her, he said, "Why boast of beating such laggards? I offer myself for the contest."

Atalanta, who found herself equally fond of Hippomenes, looked at him with pity in her eyes. She didn't know whether she wanted to beat him in the footrace or not. She hoped he would not be foolish enough to challenge her.

"What god can tempt one so young to throw himself away?" she asked herself as they waited for the signal.

But Hippomenes had a plan. He prayed to Venus, the goddess of love. "Help me, Venus, for you have led me on," he prayed.

Venus heard him and offered her assistance. In the garden of her temple grew a tree that bore golden apples. Venus plucked three of them and, unseen by anyone else, gave them to Hippomenes as he waited on the starting line. As the young lover hid them beneath his robe, Venus whispered to him what he must do.

At the signal, Atalanta and Hippomenes skimmed down the track, shoulder to shoulder. The cries of the spectators cheered Hippomenes, but his breath began to fail him, his throat became dry, and the goal was still far away. At that moment, he threw down one of the golden apples. Amazed, Atalanta stopped to pick it up.

Hippomenes shot ahead. Shouts burst forth from all sides. But soon Atalanta began to close the gap. Again Hippomenes dropped an apple. Atalanta paused to scoop it up, but then drew still closer. The finish line drew near; one chance remained for Hippomenes.

"Now goddess," he said, "do not fail me!" and threw the last apple to one side.

Atalanta saw it fall and hesitated—but Venus made the apple irresistible. Atalanta chased the apple and lost the race.

So the two lovers wed, but they made a terrible mistake: They were so full of their own happiness that they forgot to pay honor to Venus, who brought them together. The goddess, deeply hurt, plotted her punishment. Hippomenes and Atalanta were changed into a lion and lioness, and that is how they lived out their days.